Russell AND THE LOST TREASURE

Rob Scotton

SCHOLASTIC INC.
New York Toronto London Auckland
Sydney Mexico City New Delhi Hong Kong

A special thank-you to Maria

—R.S.

ISBN 978-0-545-28099-0

12 11 10 9 8 7 6 5 4 3 2 1   10 11 12 13 14 15/0

Printed in the U.S.A.   08

This edition first printing, September 2010

Typography by Martha Rago

For John H. and Livvie

—R.S.

he was distracted by a passing crow.

"Wow, a treasure map!" exclaimed Russell.

Russell fell to the ground with a thud—
and a really good idea.
   "I will find the Lost Treasure of Frogsbottom!"

So Russell went to his workshop, and after much banging
and clattering,

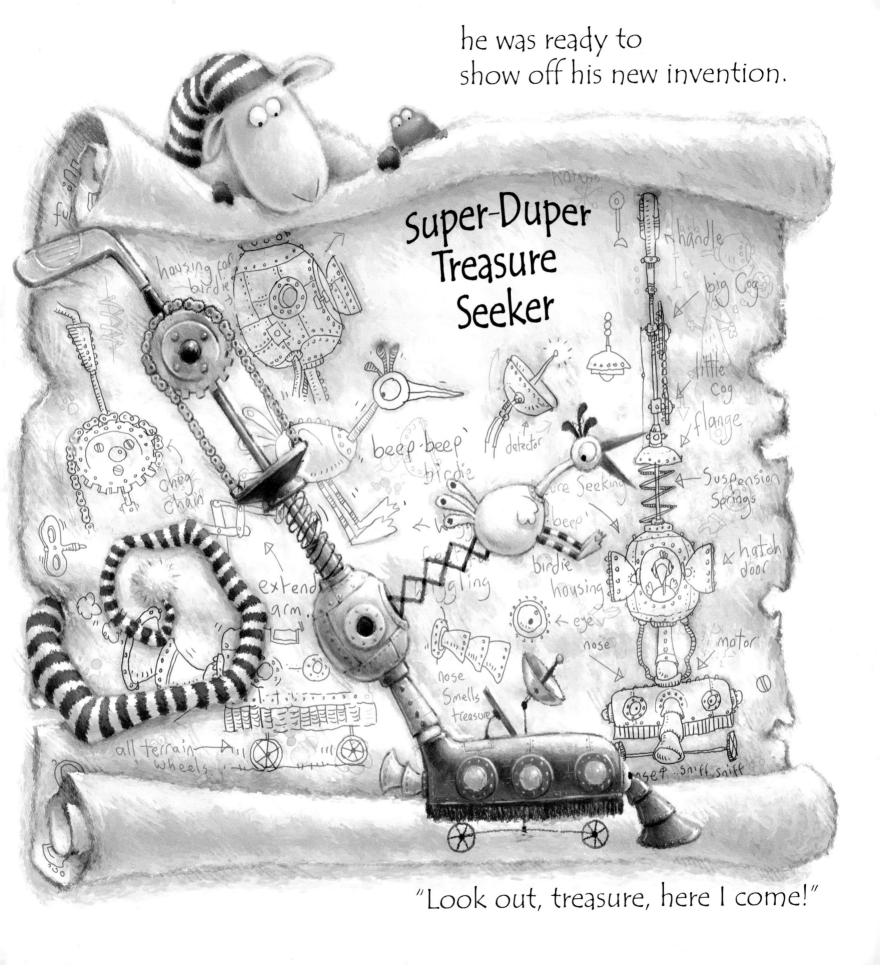

he was ready to
show off his new invention.

"Look out, treasure, here I come!"

He searched high,

he searched low.

He looked in

and out . . .

over,

under,

left

and right.   Nothing!

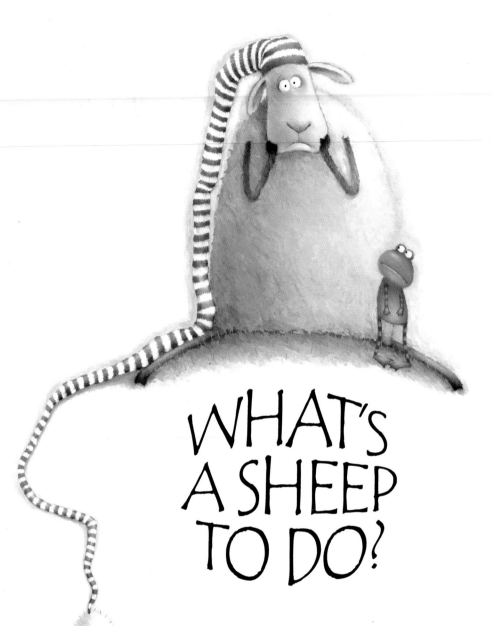

WHAT'S
A SHEEP
TO DO?

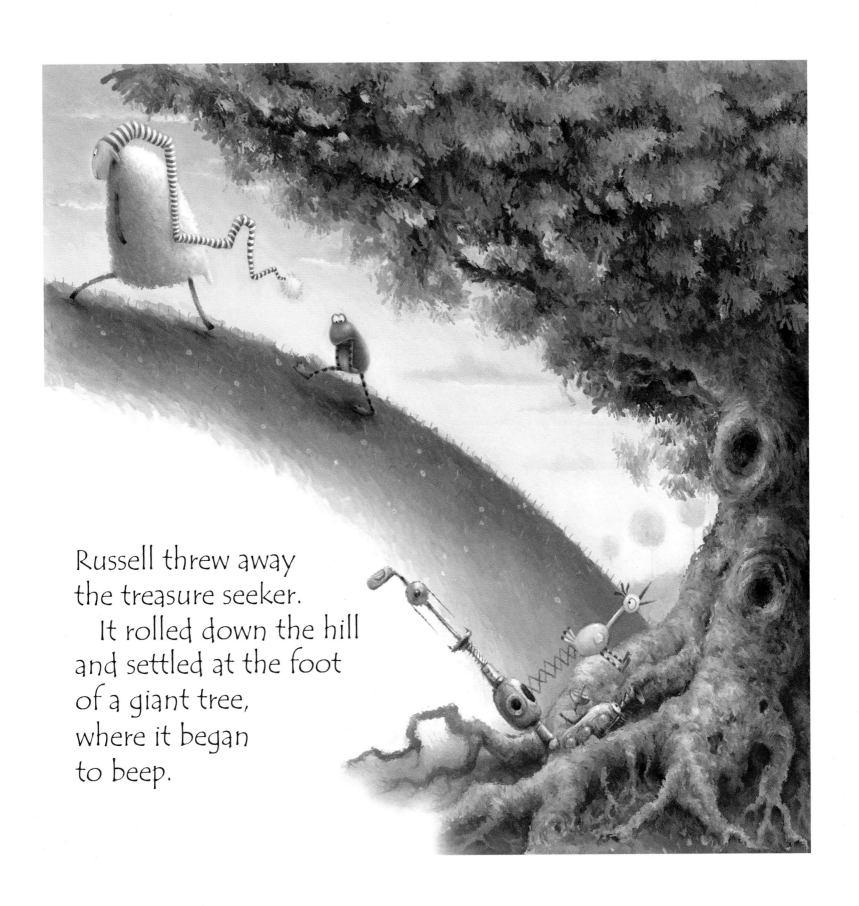

Russell threw away
the treasure seeker.
    It rolled down the hill
and settled at the foot
of a giant tree,
where it began
to beep.

Russell's hat curled with excitement.

He squeezed into a hole
at the base of the tree,

Russell dragged the chest
from under the tree,
turned the key,

and peered inside.

The chest was crammed FULL, brimming with . . .

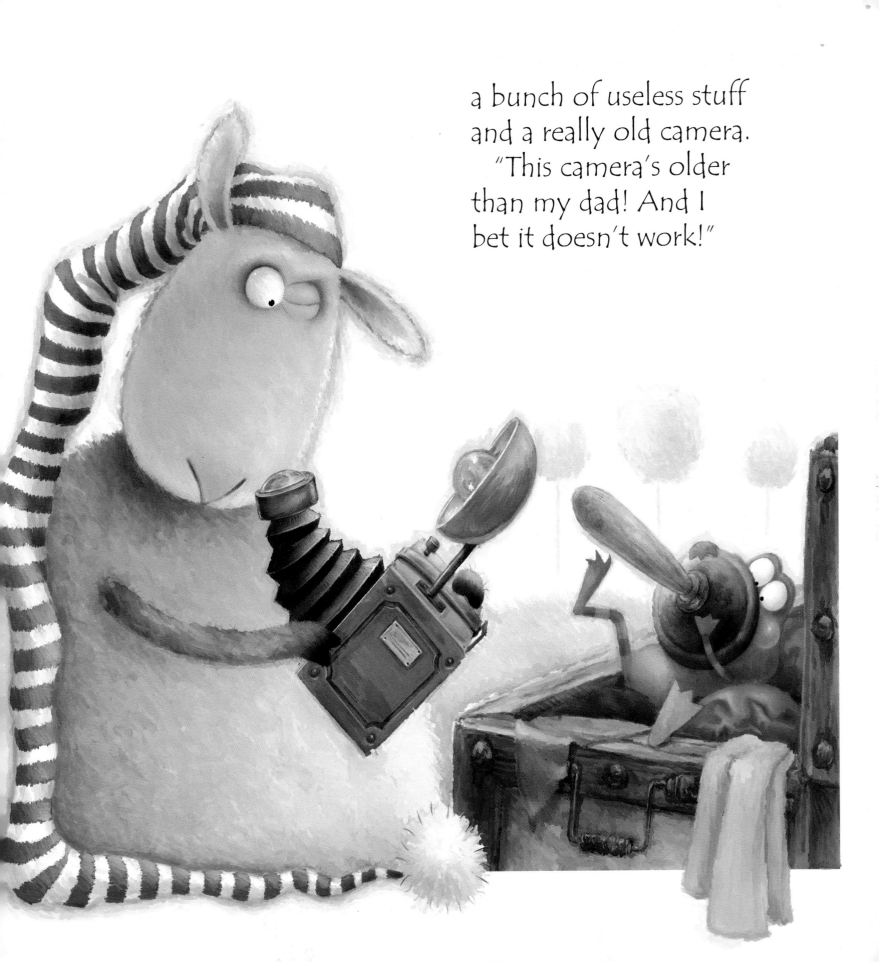

a bunch of useless stuff and a really old camera. "This camera's older than my dad! And I bet it doesn't work!"

"Then again, I bet it does!"

"There is no treasure," said Russell with a sigh. "But maybe we can have some fun anyway."

So he carefully
rummaged through the chest,

pulled out a painted sheet, and tied it between two trees.
"Mom and Dad," he called, "say 'Fleece!'"

"Granny, put your teeth in. You too, Granddad."

Flash!

Auntie and Uncle wanted a glamorous shot. "Look," said Auntie, "I'm a movie star!"

Russell's brother Cedric and the cousins wanted an action picture. "Steady, boys!"

Molly, Polly, and Dolly, the triplets, had their photo taken with their dollies—*all of them.*

Russell took Frankie's photo.

Frankie took Russell's photo.

"Cool!"
said Russell proudly.

Russell stuck the photographs into a very big book and sat down to admire his handiwork.

"Hmmm," he thought. "Maybe I have found treasure after all."

"The best treasure ever."